Nothing Better Than Gym Friends

by Melisa Torres

Illustrated by Daniel Ramos

For my AVGC girls, you know who you are,
thank you for *never ever* acting like mean girls.
Mel

Chapter 1

Back Hip Circle on Bars

The bell rings for morning recess and Megan and I sprint to the monkey bars on the playground as fast as we can. There are only three bars; if we get there first we don't have to wait.

"We're going to make it today, Savannah," Megan says, running beside me. And she's right. We are the first second grade class to get out to recess and the playground is empty. We run and jump on a bar next to each other. I do a pullover to get up on the bar and Megan hooks a leg through to get herself up. Then she starts to swing around fast with one knee hooked around the bar and I start doing continuous back hip circles. We are having so much fun spinning and spinning.

"How do you do it without your knee hooked?" Megan asks.

I stop to explain, but before I say anything someone yells out to us. "Hey, Megan! Why don't you walk with us?" Megan turns her head and there is Lily, standing with her arm hooked to Sarah's. I look at Megan, who seems startled.

Megan looks at me, shrugs, and says, "I think I'm going to walk with them for a bit. Bye Savannah."

And just like that she jumps down from the bar, runs over to Lily, and links arms with her. The three of them walk off with Sarah and Megan's heads tilted in toward Lily's to hear what she is saying.

I've stopped swinging as I watch them walk away. I don't feel like swinging anymore so I jump down. I walk over to the edge of the play area where there is curbing. I step up on the curbing, which is about the size of a balance beam, and I start walking on it and thinking. *Why wasn't I invited to walk with those girls?* If they knew me better, they would have invited me to walk with them. I'm nice and my friends at gymnastics all like me. I circle the playground area a few more times before recess is over. Playing without Megan is so boring. I can't wait for school to be over today so I can play at Trista's house.

"Then, when the bell rang and I was in line to go inside, Lily told me Megan is her second best friend and can't play on the bars with me anymore," I say.

The miserable school day finally ended and I'm next door at Trista's house telling her what happened at recess.

"Well that's stupid. Megan likes playing on the bars with you," Trista replies.

"Not anymore," I pout.

"What does Megan say about not playing on bars anymore?" Trista asks me.

"Megan doesn't say anything, I don't understand," I confess.

"Well, it's dumb. Do what you want at recess and don't worry about those girls," Trista says. I know Trista means well, but how can I do what I want if there is no one to play with?

"Anyway, we have a fun weekend coming up," Trista continues.

She's right, we have our first gymnastics meet this weekend and after the meet our teammate, Marissa, is having a birthday party.

"Are you nervous?" Trista asks me.

"Nervous about what?" I ask.

"The meet, silly!" she shrieks.

"Well, no. Don't we just do what we've been doing in practice?" I ask.

"Yeah, but people are going to be watching and taking pictures and there will be another team there, maybe two, and we want to win!" she says.

"Win?" I ask. "How do we win?" I should know this. I mean, my mom takes me to the University of Utah gymnastics meets and they always win but I'm not sure how that happens.

"We add up all our scores or something. I'm not sure," Trista admits as she flops on her bed and rolls to her tummy. She leans over her bed and puts her hands on the ground. Her straight brown hair falls upside down as she bounces to a handstand.

"All I know is," she huffs from her handstand, "that I want to be the best and I want to earn a medal." Then she lets her handstand fall onto the bed and is on her stomach again.

I look at her laying on her belly, "How do you know about medals?" I ask.

"Kayla from the gym told me. She said that at most meets you get ribbons or little medals and sometimes you get really big medals or even trophies." Trista bounces up to a handstand for a second and drops to her belly in a hollow body

11

position and bounces back up to handstand. Even though she is holding a handstand she keeps talking.

"She said big medals and trophies are more common in the higher levels like 7 and 8," Trista explains, getting a little out of breath now. She drops her handstand back to her tummy on her bed.

"Girls! Five minutes!" Trista's mom yells up to us. Trista hops up and runs over to her dresser. At the same time, I pick up the duffel bag of leotards that I brought with me.

"What leotard do you want to wear?" I ask, as I dump the contents of the duffel bag on the floor.

"I don't need one today. My mom finally bought me a new one for making Level 3."

Trista worked so hard over the summer to become a Level 3. I'm glad she did because now I have a friend and neighbor on my team.

She pulls out her new leotard and holds it up for me. The bodice is a beautiful black shimmer with zebra print on the tank shoulders and the top half of the back. Lime green piping is on the edges of the zebra print.

"Oh, Trista, that one is so fun and so you," I smile.

"I know. My mom almost didn't get it because it was so expensive. I think she finally felt bad I started wearing your leos," she says, as she steps out of her jeans and into her new leo. "Can I still borrow some workout shorts?" she asks, as she wiggles into her new leotard.

I frown at my huge pile of leotards and shorts and wonder how much it cost my mom. She buys them for me all the time. I don't have to earn them like Trista did.

"Yeah, sure," I say, and bend down to grab a pair of black shorts for her and my pink camo leo for me.

"I don't get that one," Trista says.

"What?" I ask as I toss her the shorts.

"The pink camouflage," she says catching the shorts. "What exactly are you blending in with that's pink?"

"I don't know," I say laughing, "it's just

supposed to be cute." It feels good to laugh. I haven't laughed since Lily stole Megan from me.

"Girls!" Trista's mom yells up to us. This means we need to hurry down to the car.

I guess I can't worry about Megan right now, it's time for practice.

Chapter 2

Pivot Turn on Beam

I run my hand across the beam before I
jump up. I love the feel of the rough leather and
the sensation of being so far off the ground. As I
climb up and stand to my full height, I look around
the gym. Everything looks so much different from
up here. I'm small for a seven-year-old, so I rarely

get to see things higher than other people.

"This end of the beam!" James yells. He's our gymnastics coach. I'm on a team with four other girls. We train at Perfect Balance Gymnastics Academy, also known as PBGA.

We get situated at one end of the beam and James instructs us in our beam warm-ups. "Forward walks. High relevé, arms out, chins up, knees straight, toes pointed."

We do as he says and walk on our tippy toes to the other end of the beam. When we get to the end we have to wait on our tippy toes with our arms out until he tells us to turn.

I'm sharing a beam with Trista, so I look at the back of Trista's head as I do my forward walks. Her brown hair is pulled back into a ponytail with a lime green headband. She likes the green headband because she says it makes her hazel eyes look closer to green, and today it matches her new leotard. We get to the end of the beam and stop and wait on our tippy toes. My calves are burning as I wait for James to tell us to turn.

"Arms up!" he yells, and we raise our arms to

a ballet fifth position above our heads keeping our feet also in the fifth position. "Turn!" he yells, and we do a quick pivot turn on our toes so that we are facing him, still in fifth position with the other foot in front. "Arms out, walk back," he says, even though we know to walk back toward him.

As I am walking I look over and see Marissa and Alexis sharing a beam and Paige is on the other side of them. Marissa and Alexis look like identical gymnasts on the beam next to me because they are exactly the same size and they are both wearing navy and white Perfect Balance workout leotards. They are doing their tip-toe walks in sync with each other. The only thing different about them is their coloring. Alexis has blond hair and blue eyes like me, but her hair is straight and cut in a cute A-line bob. Marissa is not as pale as Alexis with her long black hair and dark eyes.

"Red, keep your knees straight!" James calls out to Paige. James calls Paige Red because of her crazy red hair. It's curly and bouncy and always seems to be going every which way. My hair is curly, but nothing like the corkscrew curls

Paige has.

I make it to the other end of the beam and I know to raise my arms to fifth position and wait for James to tell us to walk backwards.

"Walk backwards!" James shouts out. Since we are already facing backwards we don't have to turn this time, we just position our arms to the side and walk backwards. I take this moment from high on the beam to check out what else is going on in the gym. It looks like the Level 8s are getting ready to tumble into the pit. I love watching those girls tumble; they are so good.

"Anna," James yells to me (he calls me Anna as a nick name for Savannah), "stop looking around and look at the end of the beam. Eyes down, chin up, arms out." I snap my head back and watch the beam in front of me. I need to think about what I'm doing. After all, we have a big super-serious meet on Saturday.

Chapter 3

Double Back on Floor

"Did you see Kayla throwing double backs on floor today?" Trista asks me as we pile into my mom's car. "And how Katie spots so fast? It's so cool, I can't wait until we're big and can try stuff like that."

"I know, and her music is awesome. But every time I stopped to watch her, James got mad at me," I say.

"You have to be sly, Savannah. Just take quick looks between turns," Trista advises.

"Are you girls ready for Saturday?" my mom asks.

"Yes!" we both say.

"What event are you most excited about?" my mom asks Trista, even though we know the answer. Trista loves floor because she came to PGBA with tumbling experience and she is so much better than the rest of us on floor.

"Floor," Trista answers predictably. "Although James was saying today that I need to clean up the dance parts of the routine and that I won't be the best with just a good round-off back handspring."

"That's interesting," my mom says. "It's a good thing you girls practiced your routines in the yard all summer."

"What are we going to do now that it's getting cold outside?" I ask. I look at the trees as we are driving by and some of them have started to turn yellow. Even though fall has barely begun, I already miss summer. Trista and I would play outside on the grass judging each other on our gymnastics routines. Since school has started we have only played gymnastics on the grass once.

My mom chuckles, "You guys are probably too busy with school now anyway to play like you did this summer. But I saw on the weather forecast that it will be nice this weekend. You might get one more day out on the grass."

"What event are you looking forward to?" Trista asks me.

"Bars," I answer honestly.

"Ugh, I don't understand how you like bars so much. Such an annoying event," Trista complains.

"You'll get it soon Trista. Didn't you just get your front hip circle?" I ask. I thought I saw her doing that today.

"Yeah," she grins. "I can do it if I bend my knees at the end to make it around."

I can't remember how I learned a front hip circle. I just swung around like James told me to and made it. Bars has always been easy for me to do. I think it's fun and fast, unlike beam, which is slow and can be a little scary.

We get to my house, which is only two houses down from Trista's. My mom parks in the garage and Trista and I get out of the car.

"See you at school tomorrow," Trista yells over her shoulder, and she runs to the end of the driveway and over to her house. I wish I saw Trista more at school, but all we ever get to do is wave to each other when my lunch recess ends and hers begins. I wish we were in the same grade.

"Let's get you started on homework while I make dinner, okay?" my mom says to me as we walk into the house from the garage.

"Okay," I agree and climb up to the counter. She slices an apple and I munch on it while I do my math problems. I like this time when my mom is home and cooking while I do homework. I finish my subtraction worksheet before she's done making dinner. "I'm done!" I say proudly.

"Let's see," she says, turning my paper to face her. "Very good Savannah. I'm almost done making dinner so how about you draw a picture for Grandma while you wait for dinner to be ready." I agree and begin drawing a picture of a girl on bars with rainbows in the background. Wouldn't it be nice if we could do gymnastics outside? I finish the picture and set it aside to give to Grandma after school tomorrow. My mom and I sit down for a quiet dinner. It's always quiet when it's just Mom and me. I like it better when Grandma joins us for dinner. There is more talking and my mom seems happier.

"Mom?" I ask during dinner, "How do you win a meet?"

"Well, as you know, in college six girls compete and the best five scores on each event count toward the team score. The team with the highest score from all four events wins." I didn't know. I never really paid attention to the scoring at college meets. I just like watching them fly through the air.

"Is that how it will work for us on Saturday?" I ask.

"I think I remember James saying in the

team parent meeting that you only have to add up the best three scores, since the teams are smaller. I'm not certain though; we can ask him."

"It's okay, no big deal," I say quietly.

"Oh, Savannah, don't worry about it, you will do fine. You are one of the best girls on the team. This is easy for you. I can't wait to record it and show everyone."

My tummy gets a little queasy at the thought of her recording me. What if I mess up and she has nothing good to show everyone? I better work hard this week to make sure I don't mess up.

Chapter 4

Half Turn on Floor

After dinner I head up to my room. I shower, get in my night gown, brush my teeth, and wait for my mom to come in and read to me. Right now we are reading a story about magic fairies.

"Honey," my mom says, knocking on the door. I look up from flipping through the fairy book. "You got a letter in the mail."

She hands me a purple envelope with white flower stickers all over it. I tear into it and see that it's a birthday party invitation from Lily.

"It's from Lily! A party this Saturday!" I'm surprised to get an invitation from Lily, I didn't think we were friends. But maybe if I become friends with her I can play with Megan again.

"What time?" my mom asks. I hand her the invitation. She looks at it and frowns.

"What?" I say.

"It's the same time as Marissa's birthday party." I stare at my mom in stunned silence, so she continues, "Marissa? From gymnastics? Her party is after the meet," she reminds me.

"Can I go to both?" I say, with my biggest eyes I can create.

My mom laughs and says, "That look will not change the time and day of the parties. You're going to have to decide which one to go to."

"But that's impossible!" I protest. "Marissa has been talking about her party for weeks and it sounds so fun," I whine.

"Then go to Marissa's party," my mom says

kissing me on the head and climbing into bed next to me for our story time.

"You don't understand. I have to go to Lily's party if I want to stay friends with Megan," I explain.

"What do you mean?" my mom asks. I know Lily is not being nice, and I don't want to admit it to my mom. I start to pick at my stuffed bunny's frayed ear. "Savannah?" my mom prompts.

"Well, Lily hasn't been letting Megan play with me this week," I confess. "And I just know that if I don't go to the party I'll never get to play with Megan." My mom frowns at this explanation.

"Honey, that's not a good reason to pick her party over Marissa's. If Megan is really your friend, she'll keep playing with you."

"You haven't met Lily," I point out.

"Who do you have the most fun with?" my mom asks. I shrug, even though I know I love going to Parents' Night Out with my teammates. "Why don't you take a few days to think about it?"

"Okay," I agree. She picks up the fairy book from my lap and flips to where we left off the night before. "You ready to read?" She asks and I nod and snuggle in for the story.

After three chapters my mom gives me another kiss on the head, tucks me in, and leaves the room. I heave a big sigh and think about the parties. I know I would have fun at Marissa's party because I know that Paige, Alexis, and Trista will be there. On the other hand, I hardly know the girls at school and maybe I should go so I can get to know them. I'm shy at school and I want to know Lily and her friends the way I know my gymnastics friends.

I squeeze my bunny tight and ask her what she would do. I drift off to sleep as I wait for her to answer.

Chapter 5

Handstand Forward Roll on Floor

"Okay ladies, last practice before the big day," James reminds us as we warm-up. I look over at Trista and she has a big grin on her face. She can't wait to compete, but I'm not so sure. I mean, I'm excited to wear our beautiful blue and white leotard, but I've been getting more and more nervous all week.

"We are going to watch each other on each event and pretend it's a meet. Let's start on vault. Go grab the mats over by the wall and set it up on this end of the tumble strip."

I hate setting up for vault, there are so many mats we have to drag over to do our vault of running, punching, jumping to handstand, and falling to a flat back. The flat back fall is the part where we need all the mats. I wish we could just leave it set up. But the power tumbling team that rotates to the tumble strip after us always clear it away. Coach James says moving mats is good for us.

We walk over to the end of the floor that is by the offices. We start dismantling a stack of 8-inchers that are up against the wall and dragging them across the tumble strip.

Paige, Marissa, Trista, and I each have a corner of a mat. Marissa and Paige are walking at the front of the mat faster than Trista and I. We accidently drop our end of the mat and start giggling.

"Hustle up girls! It shouldn't take all day!" James yells from the other side of the floor where he is pulling a mat over from beam. Paige and

Marissa keep dragging the mat, leaving Trista and I standing empty-handed. Trista looks at me and shrugs.

"Should we just get another one?" she asks me. I nod and we head back to the stack of mats to pull another one to take over to the tumble strip. We need four total, plus the spring board, which is even harder to move.

"Trista?" I say, as we start dragging the mat along the red tumble strip.

"Yeah?" she says, adjusting her grip on the mat.

"You remember my friend Lily from school?" I ask.

"The one who runs the second grade and got Megan to stop playing with you?" she questions, raising her brown eyebrows.

"Well, yeah," I admit.

"What about her?" she asks with a huff as we struggle with the mat.

"I was invited to her birthday party," I say tentatively.

"Then go, show her you should never be

ignored. Plus, you might get some cool bracelet or something out of it in the goodie bag," she says.

"It's on Saturday. After the meet," I say as we pull the mat up onto the other three mats already stacked in place.

"What's Saturday after the meet?" Alexis asks as she and Paige help us adjust the mat on top of the others.

"Marissa's birthday party," Trista says looking at me. In that moment I know Trista can tell I'm thinking about not going to Marissa's party. I'm a little ashamed. Maybe if I hadn't complained about Lily then Trista wouldn't be looking at me like that.

James walks up with the spring board and sets it down in front of the mats. "Enough chatting time ladies; go line up for vault," he orders, ending the conversation. Thank goodness.

Chapter 6

Straight Jump, Straight Jump on Beam

"How was practice?" my mom asks as soon I hurry in the door. Trista's mom drove me home and I got cold running from the driveway to the house. I didn't wear anything over my leotard and shorts to keep warm. It was so nice out when I left for practice that my grandma and I didn't think to have me wear a sweatshirt. But the evenings are getting cold and I better start remembering to grab a hoodie.

"Good. Well, okay," I reply.

"Why just okay?" she asks.

"Well, something weird happened on beam," I admit.

"Weird? Like what?" she prompts.

"I kept falling on beam. On my handstand, on my straight jump, on everything. I never fall," I say looking at my hands. I have a new rip, but that's not bothering me nearly as much as my terrible beam workout. And the meet is Saturday. We don't have workouts on Thursday or Friday, so this was it. My last chance practice before a meet.

"Honey, you are allowed to make mistakes. It doesn't mean anything. It just means you had a bad day. You'll do fine on Saturday."

I climb up to the counter and open my backpack to pull out my worksheet for the day. "Can I go to PNO on Friday to practice one more time?"

My mom stops chopping veggies and looks at me. "Parents' Night Out will keep you up too late when you have a meet the next morning. Are you sure you need extra time?" she asks. I immediately nod that I do.

"How about Open Gym?" she asks. Open Gym is a chance for kids to work on their skills with coach supervision. It's more structured than Parents' Night Out and only gymnasts can attend. It's not as fun, but it's better than nothing.

"Yeah, I guess," I say, agreeing to Open Gym. I sulk a little as I start my homework. I'm practicing the letter S in cursive, which is fun for me since my name starts with an S.

"Okay Mopey Lou, why don't you ask Trista if she wants to go with you to Open Gym?"

This makes me light up a little. "Can I go ask her now?"

"After dinner and homework you can skip over there for a quick conversation."

I'm still in my leotard and workout shorts when I walk over to Trista's house after dinner. But this time I remember to throw on a sweatshirt. It's a cute pink one that say 'Gymnast' on it with silver stars. My mom got it for me last Christmas. I take my time walking the length of the house between us. The days are getting shorter and the sun is setting over the mountain peaks in a brilliant orange color. I love it here in Snowcap Canyon; I love the seasons. Trista has never seen snow and I can't wait to show her how to make snow angels.

I'm thinking about this as I step up to Trista's front door and ring the bell. "Hey," her sister, Madison, answers the door and yells up the stairs, "DQ, Tinkerbell is here!" Madison calls me Tinkerbell because she says I'm tiny and that I'm always wearing sparkles. I don't think it's a bad name, but Trista always tells her to cut it out.

I hear Trista thundering down the stairs, "Cut it out, Turd!" She shoves in front of her sister and shuts the front door behind her. "What's up?"

I stand there for a second. "Why does she call you DQ?"

Trista rolls her eyes, "It stands for Drama Queen."

"What's a drama queen? It's good, right? I mean, being a queen is even better than being a princess," I reason.

"No. It means I make a big deal out of *everything* and that I'm dramatic," she explains.

I can't help it; this explanation makes me giggle. Trista *does* sort of make a big deal out of everything. "Stop it," she says, but then the corner of her mouth turns up in a smirk and this makes me laugh out loud. "Savannah! I am not a drama queen!" she yells, but her indignation is lost by her own laughter.

"It's the perfect name for you! And DQ is even funnier!" Now we are both laughing harder as Trista's mom opens the door.

"You girls, what's so funny?"

"D –," I say, pointing at Trista but I can't say it. "D – ," I try again, but the more I try to stop laughing the worse it gets.

Trista gains control of herself before I do and says, "Savannah, it's not *that* funny." This only makes me laugh harder. She tries to give me a dirty look before turning to her mom. "Savannah thinks Madison's name for me, DQ, is funny," Trista explains. At this Mrs. Thompson gives a little smile.

"Savannah, I had no idea you had such a sense of humor. Or that you knew Trista so well," Mrs. Thompson comments.

"Mom!" Trista squeals, this makes me grab my stomach in laughter. Her own mom! This is great.

"Anyway, Savannah, sweetie, it's getting dark. What do you need?" her mom asks.

I calm down, which takes a minute, and ask her if Trista can go to Open Gym with me on Friday. Mrs. Thompson agrees and says she'll text my mom to figure out our rides.

"Oh, hey, Savannah," Trista says, as I am turning to go. "Can I invite Carmen? She's the Level 2 girl that was in my class over the summer."

"Sure. Bye . . . DQ," I say, skipping down the driveway.

"Savannah!" Trista yells after me, "you *cannot* use that name at the gym!" This makes me

burst into another round of laughter as I walk
home.

Chapter 7

Front Mil Circle on Bars

I cross the street in front of my school and meet up with my grandma on the corner. She always walks me home, even though my house is a short walk from school.

"How was school today?" she asks.

"Fine," I lie.

"What was fine about it?"

"Well, Megan still won't play with me because she's too busy being Lily's second best friend," I explain.

"Can't she be friends with both of you?" my grandma asks.

"No. Lily says Megan shouldn't do juvenile things like swing on the bars if she is going to be her second best friend."

"Sounds like if Megan knows what's good for her she'll stay away from Lily," my grandma concludes. We walk in silence for a while and I enjoy the crunch of the leaves under my feet.

"Your mom says you're going to Open Gym this afternoon," my grandma comments.

"Yeah, I want to practice beam one more time before the meet."

"Okay, well, you have just enough time to change and have a snack before you leave. I made you cookies as a Friday treat," she says.

"Which kind?" I ask as we walk up the driveway and enter the house.

"Your favorite," she says with a grin.

"Sugar cookies with M&M's?" I squeal. She nods and I run into the house and climb up to the kitchen counter as fast as possible. My grandma chuckles as she follows me in and starts serving me cookies and milk. Just as I am biting into my first cookie the doorbell rings and my grandma goes to get it.

"Savannah, it's for you," I hear my grandma say. Me? I climb down from my perch and walk around the corner to the front door. Megan is standing there.

"Hi," she says shyly.

"Hi," I say back.

"Do you want to come over and play?" she asks.

I look up at my grandma, "Can I go play?" I ask her.

"I thought you were going to Open Gym?" my Grandma asks.

"Oh yeah," I frown. "I'm supposed to go to gymnastics tonight," I explain to Megan.

"Oh, okay. Maybe we can play at Lily's party tomorrow?" she asks.

I smile, "That sounds good," I agree.

"Okay, see you tomorrow, Savannah," Megan says as she begins to walk away. Uh-oh, I just told her I was going to be at Lily's party when I haven't decided which party I'm going to yet. I really wish I could play with Megan tonight; I haven't played with her at recess all week.

"Let's finish your snack and get you ready for Open Gym," my grandma says as she shuts the front door.

"Hello, Trista, Carmen, Savannah," Katie says from behind the reception desk as we walk into the gym. "Are you three here for Open Gym and Parents' Night Out?" she asks.

"Open Gym. We can't stay for PNO because we have a meet tomorrow," Trista explains.

"That's right. First Level 3 meet of the season,

how exciting. Are you girls ready?" she asks.

"Yes, they are, but they don't believe me," Mrs. Thompson answers from behind us. "They want one more workout before tomorrow."

"Such dedication," Katie says with a smile. "Okay girls, I've got you down. You can head in. Melony is the coach tonight."

We walk over to the cubbies and put our sweatshirts and shoes away. Then we walk into the training area and over to floor to start warming up.

"So what is it you need to work?" Carmen asks as we start doing tuck jumps.

"I need to do bars, but not for tomorrow, just in general," Trista huffs, doing her tuck jumps.

The three of us stop talking for a minute while we jump. We are supposed to do 10 tuck jumps, 10 straddle jumps, and 10 split jumps to get our hearts going before we stretch in our splits. But at Open Gym we only do the tuck jumps, mostly because no one is watching.

"Why not for tomorrow?" Carmen asks, as she stops jumping and sits down.

"Because I'm not competing bars

tomorrow," Trista answers, also sitting.

"I didn't know you could skip events at meets," Carmen says.

"You can, but you have to be able to do all the events to move up to the next level. So I can't skip it for long," Trista explains.

"What about you, Savannah? What are you here for?" Carmen asks.

"Beam," I answer.

"Really?" Carmen asks. "I've seen you on beam. You look good to me."

"Thanks, but I'm nervous," I admit. We stretch in silence for a minute and Alexis bounces up.

"Hey guys, I'm so glad you're here. I didn't think anyone would be here with the meet tomorrow." She plops down into her right splits without doing her tuck jumps.

"Yeah, Savannah thinks she needs more work on beam and she dragged us along," Trista says. "Why are you here?"

"My choices were batting cages with my oldest three brothers or Open Gym with Drew. I obviously picked Open Gym with Drew."

"What does Drew want to work tonight?" Trista asks.

"Pommel horse. Well, the mushroom actually. He needs to work circles. Why are we talking about my stupid brother?" Alexis asks and I can see this embarrasses Trista a little as she shrugs.

Alexis turns to Carmen and says, "Do you go here?" Sometimes we meet gymnasts from other clubs trying out our gym during Open Gym.

"Yes, I'm a Level 2 here," Carmen answers.

"What are your working tonight?" Alexis asks.

"Mil circles on bars."

"Can I spot you?" Alexis asks. "I don't feel like working out for real," she confesses.

"That'd be great," Carmen says, getting up. "Let's go over to bars now before it gets too busy." With that Carmen and Alexis head over to the quad bars on the other side of the gym.

"I swear, I think Alexis likes spotting more than she likes doing," Trista comments. "But I'm glad she's helping Carmen."

"Yeah," I say, standing up. "You ready?" I

ask.

"Beam?" she asks.

"Beam," I confirm.

Trista pretended to be a judge while I did my beam routine several times. Then we went to bars and I tried to help her with her shoot through and mil circle. But honestly, I can't remember how I learned them. I can just do it. Thankfully, Alexis helped Trista with bars and she did make progress.

By the time my mom comes to pick us up we're playing on the trampoline and we're not working on specific skills anymore. I see her waving to us, trying to get our attention.

"My mom is here," I say to Carmen and Trista.

Trista does one more back flip on the trampoline and we walk over to the glass doors where my mom is waiting.

"How'd it go?" my mom asks as we walk up.

"Good," I say with a smile. "I can do beam again."

"I never doubted it, honey."

Chapter 8

Split Jump, Straight Jump on Floor

I wake up to the smell of bacon. Today is my first meet! I jump out of bed and put my beautiful PBGA team leotard on. It's shimmery navy blue with one navy sleeve and the other sleeve is white. The white continues along the neckline. There are silver snowflakes on the chest and the bottom of both sleeves. It's beautiful.

I look in the mirror. The competition leotard makes me look official, like the gymnasts on television. I do some beam poses in front of the mirror. It looks great. I even have quad muscles in my legs like Kayla.

My mom pokes her head in my room, "Good morning."

I look up with a huge grin. "Isn't it beautiful?"

"It is," she agrees. "You look adorable and I'm going to take a thousand pictures. I'm so proud of you." This makes me a little nervous. How does she know it's going to go so well?

"What did you decide about the parties today?" she asks.

"I want to go to Lily's party," I hear myself say. I'm still torn about which party to go to. Lily can be mean sometimes. And my gymnastics friends are always nice to me. But I want to have a group of friends at Hilltop Elementary like I do at PBGA. I need to go to the party so that school kids remember who I am. Besides, I'm already friends with my teammates.

"Okay, my little superstar, take that off and

jump in the shower. Breakfast is about ready."

"Okay," I sigh. I take one last look in the mirror before I get ready for real. Now I just see a little girl playing dress up instead of an Olympic Athlete.

"Good morning, Anna," Coach James says to me as I join my team on the floor at Aerial Gymnastics. James doesn't look like himself today, he looks fancier. He isn't wearing his usual black sweats with the white stripes down the side. He's wearing jeans instead. And in place of his regular Puma sweatshirt he's wearing a navy blue shirt with a collar that has the PBGA snowflake logo embroidered on the upper left. His face is clean shaven, which looks a little odd because he usually has a short beard. But what makes him look really different is that he's not wearing a baseball hat. I can see his hair and it looks like he even has hair gel in it. Seeing James dressed up tells me that this meet is a big deal even for the grown-ups.

"We're all here. You ladies know what to do: tuck jumps, split jumps, straddle jumps," he says. We are already standing in a little circle, so we start jumping where we are.

I look around as I am jumping; there are two other teams here. The floor in this gym is right in the middle with beams to one side and bars on the other. In our gym the floor is on one side, beams are in the middle, and bars are on the other side. I feel odd in a different gym.

We finish our jumps and we know to start stretching in our splits. Now that we are not so loud with all of our jumping, James starts to talk to us again. "We are going to compete in Olympic order, Capital Cup format," he says.

"What's Olympic order?" Paige asks.

"What's Capital Cup?" Alexis asks at the same time.

"Olympic order is vault, bars, beam, floor," James answers. "The host team starts on vault, which is Aerial Gymnastics. We will start on bars.

Which means we will rotate bars, beam, floor, vault. And Sandy Gymnastics will go beam, floor, vault, bars."

"What are we doing again?" Marissa asks.

"Bars, beam, floor, vault," James repeats. "Capital Cup means we warm-up an event, then compete it, then rotate. Traditional Format you warm-up all four events then compete all four events. This format is better for the athlete, but can be confusing for the parents," James explains.

"Remember to stretch your wrists," he adds as he looks around. We're sitting on the floor in a semi-circle stretching out our splits and doing bridges to stretch our backs. And, as James reminded us, we stretch our wrists too.

I switch to my left leg splits and look at my teammates: Trista, Marissa, Paige, and Alexis. We look pretty awesome all matching in our navy and white. Trista has her brown hair in a ponytail as usual, but today she curled it. And Paige has her hair up in a big bun, like I see some of older girls at the gym do. It looks really sophisticated on her and she even has a little bit of lip gloss on. Alexis has her cute bob haircut out of her eyes with a silver headband. Marissa has her long black hair in a braided ponytail that is tucked under, with a white bow. My mom put my blond hair in two French braids that meet in a curly ponytail at the base of my neck. We all look so different, yet the same. Ready to compete.

The other team that was stretching next to us stands up and I hear their coach tell them to get ready for vault. I watch them in their beautiful red and white leotards and wonder what their routines will look like compared to ours. I know we have the same routines, but will they have better form? Will they score higher? They look like they know what they're doing.

"Savannah, don't look so serious," Trista says to me. "This is going to be fun. We get to compete in front of our parents and judges and show everyone what we do in the gym." She pops up and is ready to go over to . . . well, whatever event we are warming up first. Her ponytail is bouncing; in fact, her whole body is bouncing up and down from her toes. This girl is ready, and I better get ready too.

Chapter 9

Glide on Bars

James tells us it's time to head over to bars, so I stand up and follow my team. Marissa, Paige, Alexis, and I get in line to warm-up bars. Trista stands off to the side in her warm-up sweats. I can tell that not warming up with us right now is killing her. Trista does not have all of her bars skills yet, but James decided she could be on the team anyway and sit out during the bar rotation. At the time, when Trista told me she could be on team if she scratched bars, I thought it would be no big deal. But now that I see her face, I can tell it's a big deal and I feel bad.

"Anna, your turn," James says and I walk onto the spring board. I'm not sure what I'm supposed to do. I look at him questioningly. "Do your routine Anna and get a feel for the bar. It may feel a bit different from the bars at PBGA." I do as he says and I jump to the bar and do a glide. It feels the same as the bars at PBGA. This makes me feel better and I keep going and complete my entire routine without a problem.

"Good. We have time for you to do one more. I want you to slow it down and think about your form, okay?"

"Okay," I nod.

We all take a second and third turn and

then warm-ups are over.

"This is Capital Cup, so we are going to march in to start the meet, compete bars, then go to beam. Go get your sweats on and meet me over there for march in," James says, pointing to the area where I see people gathering beyond the beam.

"Warm-ups are done already?" my mom asks, as she hands me my team jacket.

"You look great peanut," my grandma says.

"It looks like they are doing Capital Cup," Alexis' mom says as she hands Alexis her jacket.

"What's Capital Cup?" my mom asks, just as confused as we were.

"They warm-up, compete, warm-up, compete. It can be confusing, but it makes the meet move faster," Alexis' mom explains.

Just then Trista bounces up in her warm-up

uniform.

"You guys ready for march in?" she asks.

"Oh, you girls look so cute," my mom gushes. "Let me take a picture before you run off." Trista puts her arms around Alexis and me and my mom snaps the picture. This picture moment makes me nervous and I feel my stomach get queasy.

"Come on," Trista says and we start to walk over to James.

"How does your mom know what Capital Cup is?" I ask Alexis.

"She did gymnastics as a kid," Alexis answers.

This stops Trista, "Really? How far did she get?" Trista asks.

"She competed for BYU, so Level 10, I guess," Alexis shrugs.

"Alexis! That is so awesome your mom was a Level 10! How come you never told us?" Trista squeals.

"I don't know; she's just my mom," Alexis answers as we reach James.

"Line up here," James says. My stomach

sinks a little as I see the other competitors in their beautiful warm-up uniforms. Maybe this isn't going to be as awesome as I thought.

Chapter 10

Front Hip Circle on Bars

"This is so awesome," Trista says. I look at her and she has a huge smile as she watches all the competitors swarming around trying to get organized into three lines.

Coaches are trying to get the three teams lined up in alphabetical order. We are first, then Sandy Gymnastics, then the home team goes last, even though Aerial Gymnastics starts with an 'A'.

We are instructed to line up shortest to tallest by team. Since I am the shortest on PBGA I will lead my team marching in. The coach from the home team comes and talks to me and tells me I am going to be the very front of all the teams for march in. Then she asks if I know what to do.

"No, this is my first meet," I confess.

"James, can I take your little one for a second and show her where to walk for march in?" she asks.

"Of course," he replies, and she takes my hand.

"You are going to lead the teams between these mats over to the back of the floor. Walk all the way to here then turn at the third tape and lead your team down this way. Stop at the edge of the floor in front of the parents." I nod and she looks at another girl she grabbed from Sandy Gymnastics. "You peel off a few feet before at the second tape. Your tape is right here," she says, pointing to a white piece of athletic tape on the floor. "Lead your team this way and have them turn and walk toward the parents," she instructs.

"Okay," we both say. Except now I have something else to worry about at this meet. It doesn't make much sense to me that the littlest kids have to lead the march in.

I go back to where all the girls are chatting and waiting to march in. I stand off to the side watching all the commotion. Trista, Marissa, and Alexis are lining up back-to-back trying to figure out who is taller so they know how to line up.

"You three are exactly the same, just line up behind Savannah," Paige says.

"No way, I'm totally taller than these two," Trista insists.

Paige observes them, "Marissa is a tad smaller than you two. But you guys are exactly the same," she says to Trista and Alexis.

"Oh, hey, Savannah," Marissa says to me, "right here, in front of me," she motions.

I walk over and stand in front of Marissa. Alexis and Trista get behind her. Paige stands there for a second assessing if we got the height order right.

Then she looks at me and says, "You'll be

fine." She must have seen my serious expression. I look down a little embarrassed I'm so transparent.

"Besides," she continues, "you're so little, if you mess up everyone will just laugh and think it's cute." This doesn't help, I don't want to be laughed at. Paige sees that I'm still scared and gets more serious. "Anna, if you go the wrong way, I'll run up and grab your hand and help you, okay?"

"Okay, thanks Paige," I say with relief.

Just then the march in music starts. "Show time," Paige says and hustles to the back of our little line. In front of me I see the meet director motioning for me to start. I lift my chin and start marching with straight arms, extended legs, and pointed toes.

All the girls in the meet follow me out on the floor. As I step onto the blue mat, the parents start clapping. Wow, they really like us! Phones from proud moms and dads are held up as they are taking pictures and recording us. I walk along the back of the floor and turn where I see the third tape. Then I walk toward the parents sitting on a small set of bleachers. The other teams behind me walk along the back of the floor and turn at their tape mark and walk toward the parents too. When we are done walking in there are three teams facing the parents. When the home team finishes lining up in their row the music stops. The meet director steps forward to announce the meet on a microphone.

"Welcome to our Level 3 Fall Classic. From Snowcap Canyon we have Perfect Balance Gymnastics Academy." When she says our name we all raise our right arm straight up and lift our chin in a salute and the parents clap.

"From Sandy, Sandy Gymnastics." The Sandy Gymnastics girls raise both arms in a salute.

"And our host team, Aerial Gymnastics." This team saluted like we did and I wonder which way is better? Or is there a way it is supposed to be?

Then the meet director introduces the judges who are all wearing a navy blue suit with a USA Gymnastics patch on the front. They look so important and official . . . and scary.

Then the announcer asks all the parents to

stand while they play the National Anthem. Listening to the National Anthem makes my stomach nauseous. It's so official. So much like the college meets. When the song is over the meet director starts talking again.

"For all our teams," the announcer continues, "this is the first meet of the season. And for many of our gymnasts this is their first competitive experience. Let's be very supportive of all our athletes, and please remember no flash photography."

"Gymnasts, march to your first event." *What? March where? We didn't practice where to go after the march in.*

Then I hear Paige, "Savannah," I look back at her. She's leaning out of the line, pointing over to bars, "walk us to bars, okay?"

I smile with relief and start walking over to bars and my team follows me in a straight line. I'm like a momma duck with my baby ducks following me. Except momma ducks know where they're going and what they're doing.

Chapter 11

Basket Swing on Bars

James is waiting for us over by bars. He has five blue cards in his hand. "Go present yourselves to the judges and then come back." *Present ourselves to the judges?* Thankfully, Paige knows what this means and leads our group over to a table where a judge is sitting facing the bars.

"Good morning, girls," the judge says.

"Good morning," some of my teammates murmur. I don't say anything. The judge has a very organized table with note cards, writing paper, sharp pencils, water, and a girl sitting next to her with a score stand that says 0.00.

"Is this a first meet for some of you?" We silently nod.

"Well, I wish all of you luck today and this season. Have fun."

"Thank you," we say. I'm not sure if we are done, but my teammates walk back over to James, so I do too.

"Okay ladies, you each get a quick turn to warm-up on bars," he instructs.

"But we just warmed up," Marissa points out.

"Yes, but you get a quick moment on the equipment before each event. It's called a one-touch warm-up. Just do a glide to make sure the spring board is where you need it."

We all do a quick glide, and come back to sit on the side of the bars.

"Alright, you guys are going to sit in order of competition. We'll change the order up for each event. Who wants to go first this time?"

No one volunteers. We look at each other,

hoping someone else will want to go first. "I can go first this time," Paige says slowly. I can tell she doesn't really want to go first, but none of us do either. I exhale, relieved Paige volunteered.

"Paige it is. Then Alexis, Savannah, and Marissa," James says as he shuffles the blue cards, putting them in some sort of order. "Sit in that order so you remember who's up next. Trista you sit on the end." The girls start shuffling around to sit in the order he called out, except I can't remember who I'm after.

"James, I don't remember who I'm after," I squeak. He smiles. "Good thing your teammates have got you covered," he says as he walks over to the judges table and gives her the blue cards. I look around and we are sitting in a straight line, and apparently, we're in order. That means I'm after Alexis.

James talks to the judge for a couple of seconds and then comes back to us. "Okay ladies, to keep this meet moving you have to be ready to go as soon as the teammate in front of you dismounts. You wait for the judge while she tallies the score. It's better for you to wait for her than the other way around." We nod and Paige stands up and walks over to the low bar.

She waits by the spring board like we were taught in practice. Except that was different because James was pretending to be our judge, this judge is a stranger.

"Paige?" the judge says. Paige nods and the judge smiles and raises her arm to indicate to Paige that she is ready to watch her routine. Paige smiles back and raises her arms to indicate she is ready and her routine is beginning. She gets up on the spring board, starts with a glide, then her pull over, right into her front hip circle. She is doing a great job. This makes me relax a little.

I hear clapping from the other side of the gym and I see that the host team had a girl just finish a vault and I guess the parents are happy with her. Then I look over and see a girl competing on beam. A lot is going on at once. I hear my teammates clapping and I realize I just missed the second half of Paige's routine. She is smiling and bounding over to us. I assume it went well.

"Great job!" Alexis says, and so I tell her great job too.

"Thanks!" Paige is grinning and anxiously turns to look for her score. I see that Alexis is already standing by the spring board ready to start her routine. James wasn't kidding when he said we had to be ready. The judge is looking down and not even looking at Alexis. She is figuring out Paige's score. Then she hands one of the blue cards to the girl sitting next to her.

And before the girl does anything with that blue card the judge looks up and says, "Alexis?" Alexis nods and the judge smiles and raises her arm to show she is ready, Alexis raises her arms to salute that she is ready and she begins her routine.

Meanwhile I hear Paige whispering, "7.60, that's good, right?" I turn and see the girl sitting next to the judge has made the numbers on her stand say 7.60 for Paige's score. While Trista is congratulating Paige, I decide going first is better because then you can be busy celebrating instead of being nervous.

Alexis is competing her bar routine and I pay

attention to her so I don't miss when I am supposed to walk over and be ready for my routine. Alexis finishes her routine with a clean dismount and I stand up and make my way over to the springboard. James gives Alexis a high five and then walks over to me.

"Savannah?" James asks.

"Yeah?" I squeak.

"This is supposed to be fun." I blink at him. "You know, fun? Smile and breathe." I let my breath out in a whoosh. He laughs and says, "Just do what you do in practice and you'll be fine." He pats me on the shoulder and steps to the side. I see the judge is looking at us and that she is ready for me.

"Savannah?" She looks at me expectantly. I nod and give a half smile. She raises her arm and then I raise my arms in a salute.

I climb up to the spring board. *Do what I do in practice, do what I do in practice*. I can do that. I jump into my glide. After the glide I stop and pull myself to my chin and lift my feet up and over in a perfect pull over. I stop and do my front hip circle.

As I am coming around on my front hip circle, I am feeling better. I feel more like I'm at Perfect Balance.

Then I do my shoot through, mil circle, basket swing, and I pause to cut my front leg over so I am back in a support position. I do all these skills just like I do in practice. Next I cast as high as I can into my back hip circle, remembering to keep my legs together and straight and my toes pointed. I immediately swing down into my dismount. I take a little step on the landing and I'm done! I salute where I am standing with both arms up. Then I turn and salute the judge, who is smiling at me.

I can hear my mom yelling, "Great job Savannah!"

The judge smiles, says, "Thank you," and looks down at her notes. I start to bound over to Trista, but James steps in front of me.

"Great start, Anna," he says and pats me on the shoulder.

I grin at him. "Thanks," I say, and give him a high five. I walk to my team and I can feel my heart is pounding even though I'm done with my routine. My teammates all give me quick high fives before Marissa starts her routine.

I sit down, knowing I am supposed to watch Marissa's routine, but I can't seem to settle down. Blood is pumping through my body like I'm nervous, only I'm not nervous. I'm keyed up for some reason and I feel great that my routine went so well.

"You did great, Anna," I hear, and turn and see it's Trista. "Really. That was a good routine," she says.

I smile at her and Paige says, "8.20," as my score comes up, "not bad, shrimp."

What was I worried about? This is great! Competing is so fun!

Chapter 12

Rond de Jambe to Arabesque on Beam

"Solid start ladies," James says to us when we are done competing bars. "Beam is next. We have to wait for beam to finish competing and then we'll head over there."

I look over to the beams and see a girl is, in fact, competing. I watch her kick up into a perfect handstand for her dismount.

"Are you excited for beam?" I ask Trista.

"Yes! It was hard to sit out. I'm ready for the

other events."

Just then the meet director's voice comes over the loud speaker. "Gymnasts, that concludes our first rotation. Please march to your next event." I start to scramble for my warm-up jacket and pants.

"Just grab them, Savannah, you don't have to put them on. We can walk to beam in our leotards," Paige says, scooping up her jacket and pants. "Take us to beam, shrimp."

Me? I have to lead again? My teammates are all lined up in order of height waiting for me to get to the front of the line. I hustle to the front and wonder which way to go. I see the lonely beam standing on the other side of the gym. I decide to walk how I was taught in our gym, between the equipment. I walk between the edge of the spring floor and the vault runway and over to beam. As we are walking, I hear my mom cheering. "Looking good PBGA!"

When we get to the edge of the mat that sits under the beam, James rounds us up into a huddle. "Okay ladies, you are going to warm-up in the order you are going to compete.

"Who wants to be first this time?" James asks.

"Me!" Trista raises her hand and bounces up and down.

"Okay. Trista, then Paige, Marissa, Savannah, and Alexis."

"You are going to jump up in the order I just put you in for warm-ups. Each person gets 30 seconds, which is plenty of time up there to get comfortable. I want you to walk through your routine. Do all the major skills the direction you will do them in the meet. Got it?"

"Yes," we nod in agreement even though I am not sure what walking through a routine means.

James looks over at the girl sitting next to the judge. She is holding a stop watch. "Ready?" she says.

"Ready," James says and looks over at Trista. Trista jumps up and does exactly what James says. I see that walking through a routine means you can skip the dance poses.

"Ten seconds," the timer girl says. Trista

hurries over to the middle of the beam for her dismount. Paige jumps up next without a word and does exactly what Trista just did. Then it's Marissa's turn. After she does a few skills the timer yells, "Time!" Marissa jumps down and I know it's my turn to climb up.

I quickly climb up on the beam. I stand all the way up. It looks weird and scary up here, not at all like at PBGA. I walk over to the section of the beam where my handstand will be. I do my handstand, and as I step down out of my handstand my legs are shaking. When my feet touch I can feel I am off to the side a little. I lift my chest to complete the handstand and I fall off the beam. *Oh no!* I quickly jump up and try again. I do my handstand, and my feet connect back down on the beam, but as I stand up, I fall. I jump up again and I hear James say, "Anna, no more handstands. Do your other skills."

I nod and prepare for my leap. Just before I go I hear, "Ten seconds!" from the timer girl. *Ten seconds? I better hustle.* I rush through a tiny leap, stretch jumps, and then I fall on my half turn. As I am climbing up to try again James says, "Jump down Anna, your time is up."

This is *not* fun.

I had a terrible warm-up. I didn't even warm-up my dismount.

"Anna, you're dropping your chest as you come up from your handstand. Your handstand is straight, but dropping your chest is making you fall. If you keep your arms by your ears and spot the end of the beam, you will come up straight. Okay?"

"Okay," I say. *What did he just say?*

I'm trying not to panic as Alexis finishes her beam warm-up.

"One more time through," James says and Trista jumps up on the beam. James looks down at me, "Next time up there I want you to do your turn and dismount." I nod in agreement, although I would like to do another handstand.

When it's my turn, I do as James says. I execute a timid turn, but at least I make it. Then I walk over to where my dismount will be and I kick up into a handstand and turn into the dismount.

As soon as I land Alexis jumps up for her last turn. I back away from the beam, wishing I had one more turn.

As soon as Alexis dismounts James says, "Warm-ups are over ladies, present yourself to the head judge and then come talk to me."

We nod and head over to the judge that is by the score stand. "Hi, girls," the judge smiles. She looks so official in her navy suit with the USA Gymnastics patch. It scares me, but at the same time, she seems nice.

"Hi," we say together, less shy than over at bars.

"How was bars?"

"Great! The whole team hit all their skills!" Trista replies enthusiastically.

How does Trista know that? The rotation went too fast for me, I didn't see all of my teammates' routines.

"Glad to hear it," the judge replies. "Ready for beam?"

"Yes," we say.

"Okay, good luck." We thank her and go

back to James. James has us sit on the edge of a mat in the order we are competing. He walks Trista over to the beam and is talking to her while they wait for the judge to salute her. I'm excited for Trista. She has worked so hard for this chance. James backs away from Trista and the judge salutes her and she salutes back.

Trista turns to the beam, swings her leg up in the mount and stands up gracefully. She is poised up there and does not seem nervous at all. She looks really cute in our navy and white leotard. She performs a perfect handstand. I hope mine looks like that. Then she does her arabesque, her leap, jumps, pivot turn, half turn, and her dismount. All with no problem. Just like in practice. Better than practice. My stomach sinks and my heart starts pounding. I don't think I can do mine like that.

"Can I go to the bathroom?" I ask James as Trista bounces over. He quickly nods to me and turns his attention back to Trista. I stand up and walk past Paige who is standing next to the beam waiting to compete next. I start to walk to the bathroom, but I end up walking over to my mom.

"What's wrong, honey?" my mom says to me when I walk up.

"Their beam is different," I blurt out. "Everything looks different from up there. And it's all by itself."

"What do you mean, all by itself?" she asks.

"Well, at Perfect Balance, there are four beams next to each other. But here they moved all their beams over to that wall and left only one standing all alone. There's so much space around it. It feels lonely," I try to explain.

"They did that for the meet, so everyone can see you better."

"It just feels weird," I say.

"Honey, just do your best, okay?" She smiles at me and my butterflies come back.

"Hey, Houdini," I hear Paige say as she walks up to us. "James says you need to come back over to beam." Paige puts her arm around me and says to my mom. "I guess we're not supposed to talk to our parents during competition." Paige turns me away from my mom and walks me back to the beam area. I'm embarrassed Paige had to come get me and now I feel bad I missed her routine.

"How did your routine go?" I ask.

"I wobbled a lot, but I stayed on. I got a 7.35," she answers.

I don't say anything.

"It's okay, Anna," Paige says. "You'll be fine when it's your turn. Pretend you're in our gym at practice."

I nod. But this doesn't really help because I've never been nervous in practice. And we don't practice on such a lonely beam. And at practice there's no judge just waiting for me to mess up. And my mom isn't watching with her phone out, ready to put my routine on Facebook.

How can I possibly pretend this is practice?

Chapter 13

Cross Handstand on Beam

By the time we get back to the beam area Marissa is done with her routine and I am up next.

"Thank you Paige," James says when we walk up. "Savannah, you cannot disappear like that during competition. You need to stay here with your team so you can stay focused. If you need something, you come to me. Okay?" I nod silently and feel stupid. I didn't mean to disappear, I just needed to talk to my mom.

"Savannah, listen to me. You are a talented

little gymnast and beam is a piece of cake for you. Just enjoy being up there and show us what you've got." He gives my shoulders a little squeeze. I nod. "Breathe," he says. I let out a breath and he chuckles. "Gotta love first meets," he mutters to himself and walks away. He leaves me standing by the lonely beam to wait for the judge all by myself.

What did he tell me to do to correct my handstand? I've heard that correction before in the gym. *Think Savannah. Think. What do I do? Chest is dropping, keep it up. Okay. And breathe, he told me to breathe. I can do that.* I take a deep breath as I watch the judge write her notes on Alexis' routine.

I feel nauseated as I step closer to the beam. This event is terrible. I look across the gym; my mom is ready, holding up her phone to record my routine. She catches my eye and winks. I give a little half smile and quickly look back at the judge. My hands are sweaty. *Why are my hands sweaty? What if I slip during my handstand because my hands are sweaty?* I quickly try to wipe them on my legs. Just then the judge passes the blue card to the score girl and turns her attention to me.

"Savannah?" she asks. I nod and she smiles
and raises her hand to me. I salute her back with a
weak smile and turn around to face the beam. I
jump up and swing my leg over in my mount and
stand up gracefully like James taught me. I do one
dance pose and I'm to my handstand. *Don't drop
my chest, don't drop my chest.* I step into my
handstand and do the tiniest handstand I have
ever done. My feet don't come up over my head
in an actual handstand. I step down and am
happy my feet touch down on the beam. But as I
come up I can feel my chest dropping, and my
balance going off to the side. All of a sudden I feel
myself falling off the beam. My feet hit the mat
with a loud thud.

My heart sinks to my stomach. I stand there
on the mats with the beam in front of me.

I fell.

I'm in a meet and I fell.

Now what? A little voice in my head says,
Get back up and finish. I climb back up and as
soon as I stand all the way up all I can think about

is how I want off of the stupid beam.

I rush through my lunge pose and my arabesque. I wobble during the arabesque and almost fall again. I rush into my leap and I can feel it is a miniature leap. Then I do my stretch jump, stretch jump, and I wobble between the two jumps, not connecting them. *I want off this beam! Pivot turn, half turn and I'm done.* I do the pivot turn fine and the half turn quick and sloppy. At least I'm down to one pose and the dismount.

I rush through the pose and the dismount. I don't hit or hold the handstand in my dismount and I know my dismount will have a lot of deductions too. But I don't care. *It's over.* My feet hit the ground and I turn and salute the judge. She smiles nicely back at me and James is already by my side. He gives me a hug and puts his arm around my shoulder.

"Okay, you got through your first beam competition. You did the right thing, you got back up and finished," he says giving my shoulder a squeeze.

That was a disaster. I messed up every skill. I

can feel a lump forming in my throat. Oh my gosh, I'm going to cry. "Anna, breathe," he instructs. I try to get a breath out, but if I do I'm going to cry. I can feel the tears forming in my eyes. "Oh, Anna, it's okay. Just a first meet. We have two more events to go, you can't fall apart now." I nod, but I can still feel my eyes stinging.

"Go to the bathroom, wipe your eyes, breathe, and forget about beam," he orders. "Paige, take her to the bathroom. Don't let her talk to her mom, and meet us at floor." Paige nods and he turns away from us to go talk to Alexis who is already standing by the beam waiting for her turn.

Paige grabs my hand and walks me away from the beam area to the bathroom. We go the long way around the floor because girls are competing on floor and I see she is avoiding the parent area.

We get to the bathroom and my tears start to fall. Paige hands me some toilet paper for my eyes. "Okay, shrimp, what happened?"

"I don't know!" I choke out. We don't say anything for a minute because now I am really crying and I can't speak. She is quiet while she waits for me to come up with a better answer than 'I don't know.'

I breathe out a few times to try to calm myself and get my tears to slow down. "It was scary up there," I finally mange. "And lonely. And I messed up warm-ups and I couldn't do it."

"First of all, you can do it," she says firmly looking me in the eye. "So you made mistakes, so what?"

"So, it was embarrassing!" I wail.

"Yeah," she agrees, "It is embarrassing and scary. I'm embarrassed that I wobbled so much and that I'm so tall."

"You are?" I sniff.

"Yeah, but I like it anyway. Are you having a little bit of fun here?" she asks.

I don't know!

Bars was fun. Maybe.

"Maybe," I say.

"Okay, so now what?" she asks.

"What do you mean, now what? It's over, I messed up."

"Beam is over. The meet's not over. James said forget beam. I heard him. So let's forget beam and go back out there and do floor, okay?" *Do I have a choice?* I look at her and she is waiting for me to reply.

"Okay," I manage.

"You ready to go back out there?"

No.

"Yes," I mumble.

Chapter 14

Splits on Floor

Paige and I come out of the bathroom and walk back into the gym. We see our team is already on floor but warm-ups have not yet begun. We walk to our team and join the group quietly since James is giving instructions.

"We will do warm-ups together," he is saying. "You can each use a strip of the floor. Do one full routine to get the feel of things. I'll have your order ready when you are done," he says.

When the other girls go out on the floor to start warming up James turns to the two of us and asks, "We good?"

"I think so. We good, shrimp?" Paige asks me.

"Yeah," I lie.

"Good, start warming up," he says.

We join our team on the floor and warm-up all of our floor exercise skills.

When we finish warming up, James tells us to go say hello to the floor judge, which we do.

"Ladies," James says, "the order is Marissa, Alexis, Savannah, Paige, and Trista. Sit over here." We arrange ourselves in the order he just called out and he walks the cards over to the judge.

As Marissa waits for the judge to be ready I realize I did not see my beam score. I lean over to talk to Trista over Paige, "Hey, Trista, what'd I get on beam?"

Trista opens her mouth to tell me and Paige interrupts, "Don't worry about it, shrimp, focus on floor." Trista stops herself and looks at Paige.

"Why can't she know?" Trista asks.

"She can, after the meet," Paige insists.

"I'm not a baby, I can handle it," I say. Although, maybe I did act like a baby.

"Yeah, she's not a baby," Trista repeats.

"Are you guys watching Marissa, or being lame teammates?" Paige asks. That shuts us up and we watch the end of Marissa's routine.

Marissa finishes a solid routine and Alexis jumps up and walks to the side of the floor to wait her turn. Alexis performs a clean floor routine; just like we do in practice. Of course, you can't fall on floor like you do on beam. Maybe floor is my new favorite event. No falling involved. I mean, you can fall out of your skill, but not off the actual apparatus. I'm thinking about this as I walk to the side of the floor.

James walks over to me. "Fierce Anna. You're a great little gymnast. Show those judges what you're made of." I nod, and he grabs my hands and squeezes them. "Have fun." Then he is gone as fast as he came. I see the judge is waiting to catch my eye.

"Savannah?" she asks. With butterflies in my

stomach I nod, salute, and walk onto the floor.

I'm standing all alone on the floor waiting for my music. I didn't think it was possible to feel more alone than on beam. But standing here in my starting pose, with the entire gym quiet, and all eyes on me, it is so very lonely and scary.

The music finally begins and I lift my chin and begin my arm movements. Next my leg swings and split jump, stretch jump. I start to feel like I do in practice. I kick over into a bridge and kick back over trying to keep my legs as straight as possible, but I know they bend just a little.

Then I kick up into a handstand and do what feels like a perfect handstand forward roll. I can hear my mom yelling as I run into my leap. This is kind of fun. I do my backward roll to push-up position and realize I am ahead of the music. I'm not sure what to do so I keep doing the dance moves and when I slide into my splits I decide to hold it for a second to wait for the music. While I wait, I smile and look up at my mom and she goes nuts clapping and yelling. This makes me giggle as I rotate into my middle splits and complete the dance moves that get me back up to my feet.

All I have left is the half turn and the round-off back handspring. I easily complete the half turn and pause for a second to wait for the music again before the round-off back handspring. I focus on squeezing my legs together during my tumbling pass and I can hear James yelling, "Great job, Anna!" as I complete the rebound and step back to my knee for the ending pose.

As soon as the music ends I pop up to my feet and salute the judges. That was so awesome! I did it! I did a routine just like in practice; maybe even better than practice!

I run over to James for a big high five. My heart is pounding and my blood is pumping fast. I feel great! I can feel a giant grin on my face.

"I knew you were fierce, little Anna," James says, giving me a quick hug. Then he turns me to my teammates. I bounce over to where they are sitting and I get a quick high five from each of them.

I sit down, but my heart is still racing and my body is jittery. I try to focus on Paige, who is talking to James and waiting to go next.

I turn to watch the judge. She finishes writing notes on my routine and passes the score card to the girl who will post the score for everyone to see. The judge salutes Paige and I don't turn to watch Paige begin; I'm too busy watching what the girl with the score card does.

As Paige starts her routine, I see my score come up as an 8.15. Is that good? I don't know. I look to my teammates to see if an 8.15 is good, but none of them have seen my score. They are watching Paige. I look over at my mom. She sees me and gives me a thumbs up. I wave to her.

I hear the music stop and I whip my head around to pretend like I was watching Paige. I high five her when she walks over to us with James.

"Great floor set, ladies, let's sit back and enjoy watching Trista kill it." This routine is easy for Trista. And man, she knows it. She is grinning ear-to-ear as she walks to the edge of the floor and waits for the judge to salute her.

As James predicted, Trista does a beautiful routine. She looked even better than in workout.

"Whoo-hoo, that was fun!" Trista says, as she bounds over to us after her routine.

"Grab your sweats, ladies, and head to vault," James instructs.

We haven't even seen Trista's score yet, but we are supposed to be marching over to vault. I can tell she is stalling by fiddling with her sweats so she can see her score before we leave floor. I walk over and put my arm around her. The judge hands the girl sitting next to her the blue card, she looks at it and starts to put a score up. She puts the score up and then turns it toward us. 8.5! Wow, an 8.5! That's great! We squeal together and I find I am bouncing on my toes just as Trista is doing.

Chapter 15

Handspring to Flat Back on Vault

"Savannah, we need you to get us over to vault," Paige says, interrupting our little celebration. Paige is right; the other teams are marching to their next event. I scamper over to the front of the line that Paige, Alexis, and Marissa have formed with Trista right behind me. *This meet isn't so bad after all,* I think, as I lead my team over to vault. All we have left is vault and vault is easy.

"Who wants to go first?" James asks as we get over to the vault area. Trista and I both raise our hands and James starts laughing. "This is a nice change from the beginning of the meet. Okay, Savannah, you're up first since you haven't started us off yet. Then Trista, Marissa, Alexis, and Paige can finish up the meet for us," he says.

We line up to do our warm-up vaults. Since I am first James tells me to lead the team in a few practice runs. Then we each get three vaults to warm-up. I am up first. I run, hurdle, and hit the spring board. It doesn't bounce. I don't make it all the way up to the handstand and I fall back down on the board. I look up at James confused.

"This spring board is newer than ours. The springs are tighter. You're going to have to run fast and be tight when you hit the board," he says. "Get back in line and try again."

The equipment on the other events felt about the same. But this board is really different. I stand back in line and watch my teammates. They are all able to make it up to the handstand and fall to a flat back.

I stand in line behind Paige and mutter, "I hate that spring board."

Paige turns around and looks at me, "Is it a hard board?" she asks. I nod with a pouty face. "Well, you are tiny. I can really smash it because I'm bigger than you. You're going to have to work harder shrimp," she says unsympathetic.

"Well, that's not fair," I whine.

"Sure it is. The other events are easier for you because you're small. This is the one event where being bigger helps me," she says with her hands on her hips.

"Oh," I say, wondering how bars and beam might be harder for Paige. Then it's her turn to vault and I watch her run and do a perfect vault.

Then James motions to me from the spring board that it's my turn. I run, punch, and jump to handstand so slowly that I barely make it up and then I get stuck in the handstand. James reaches up and pushes my legs so I fall to a flat back.

"If that happens during competition, tuck your head in and move your toes over your head toward the mat. It will pull you over," he says. "But it would just make everything easier if you punch hard and drive your heels fast."

I nod and walk back to where my teammates are lined up. I get one more warm-up vault and two in competition. I line up behind Paige to do my last warm-up. I stand quietly since Paige is talking to Alexis who is in front of her.

I do my one last warm-up and I make it over with a very sloppy handstand. But at least I made it. I stand off to the side as I wait for my teammates to finish their third warm-up vaults.

When everyone is done James has us sit in order except me because I'm up first. He walks with me to where I will start my vault.

"Alright, you made a come-back on floor. Let's keep that momentum going," he says and gives my shoulder a little squeeze. "Fast heels," he reminds me as he backs away.

I look down to where the judges are sitting by the stack of mats. I look over at my teammates who are quietly watching me. I look up and see my mom holding up her phone.

I feel butterflies in my stomach again. *Did I*

say vault was easy? Why would I say that? It's easy at Perfect Balance because we have better spring boards. *Is there one more mat up there than I'm used to? Maybe James got the mats wrong?* The judge raises her hand stopping my thoughts.

I smile a stiff smile and lift my arms, saluting back. I start to run, hurdle, and punch the stiff board. I think about moving my heels as fast as I can off of the board as I jump into the handstand. I can feel I have enough momentum to make it over and I easily fall to a flat back. *I did it!* I sit up, salute the judges, and jump down from the mats.

James walks up with a grin, "One more like that and you've just survived your first meet," he says, high fiving me. I grin and quickly walk back to start my second vault. Now that I made my first vault, I'm not nervous for my second vault. When the judge salutes me I feel calm and happy and I salute her back. I run and punch the board just as hard and drive my heels just the same, doing a similar vault to my first one.

After I salute I walk over to James and he gives me a big hug and sends me to sit with my teammates while he talks to Trista.

I happily put my warm-ups on. I look up to the stands and see my mom waving and smiling. It feels good to be done with the meet.

My teammates compete vault quickly and I notice we are finished with the meet before the other two teams. We are dying to go talk to our parents now that we're done competing, but James says we need to stay here while the other teams are competing. So I just wave to my mom and grandma from where we're sitting.

Chapter 16

Chassé Leap on Floor

When the other teams finally finish on floor
and bars we are given a chance to see our
parents. I skip over to my mom and she gives me a
big hug.

"You did great, honey," she says.

"Thanks, Mom," I say with a grin.

"What happened on beam?" she asks. *Oh
yeah, beam*. Thinking about beam makes the
happy feeling and my smile disappear.

109

"Debbie," my grandma says in a warning tone glaring at my mom.

"I'm not sure," I say lamely.

"Well, that's okay. We'll just see if we can do some private lessons with Katie to fix that handstand," she says.

I don't really want to do a private lesson with Katie. Besides, James seems to know how to fix it. I just couldn't remember what he said. But I don't want to tell my mom that I wasn't listening to James so I don't say anything.

"I don't understand why you got such a low score when you only had one fall. There were girls from the other teams that fell three times and got the same score as you. I'm going to have to talk to James about it," my mom says.

"I think it's because I wobbled and didn't complete many of my skills," I try to explain.

"But still, you only fell once and you looked way better than those other girls," she insists. I look down at my feet because I'm not sure what to say to this.

"Let's talk about this later," my grandma

says. "Look, Trista is headed to the floor for awards, why don't you go join her," she suggests. I'm grateful to get away from my mom's questions so I smile at my grandma and scurry off to join Trista and the rest of my team for awards.

The meet director pulls out a podium awards stand. It's highest in the middle where it says 1st place, then it's a little lower on the right and left for 2nd and 3rd place, and on either side of 2nd and 3rd there is a spot close to the floor for 4th and 5th.

We sit down together as a group to wait for awards. James walks over to us with the blue score cards he has been passing back and forth with the judges all morning. "Solid first meet, ladies," he says, and he starts handing out the cards. He gets to me and I take the card he is holding out for me. I see that it has my name at the top and my score on each event.

Aerial Gymnastics Fall Classic
Savannah Collins
Perfect Balance Gymnastics Academy

Vault – 7.50

Bars – 8.20

Beam – 5.60

Floor – 8.15

AA – 29.45

Now I know why my mom was upset; 5.60 is pretty bad.

"Alexis," I ask, "what is AA?"

"That stands for All-Around. All of your scores added up make for an All-Around score," she answers.

"Great meet today by all of our competitors," the meet director says into the microphone. "I would like to turn your attention to floor for our Fall Classic awards."

"We are going to recognize each girl today for doing an excellent job. I'm going to start with the girls who earned a yellow ribbon on vault for scoring a 7.0 to a 7.45. When I call your name please come up here, get your ribbon and stay up here until I am done recognizing all the yellow ribbon winners."

She begins calling names and about 5 girls get up and stand in front of us to get their yellow ribbon and then smile for pictures.

"Thank you, girls." The yellow ribbon winners sit back down with their teammates.

"Now, for the white ribbon winners, scoring a 7.5 to a 7.95," the announcer says and then she starts rattling off names. I hear my name. *What do I do?* I look at Paige.

Thankfully, Paige can read my mind and she says, "Go on up there, shrimp, get your ribbon!"

I stand up and walk over to the volunteer and she hands me a ribbon. I line up with the other white ribbon winners and face my teammates. Behind my teammates are the parents in the bleachers and my mom is furiously taking pictures. I look down at my white ribbon. In gold letters it says, "Third Place, Fall Classic," with a picture of a gymnast doing a ring leap. I love it. It's so beautiful. By the time I'm done inspecting my ribbon the meet director has finished announcing the white ribbon winners and she tells us to sit down.

Then she announces the red ribbon winners, which are for 8.0 to 8.95 and then the blue ribbon winners, which are for 9.0 to 10. There was only one blue ribbon winner from Sandy Gymnastics, so the meet director has her stand on the first place spot on the podium.

The meet announcer goes through the same process for bars (I get a red ribbon), beam (no ribbon for me), and floor (red again). As we are clapping for a girl from Aerial Gymnastics who won a blue ribbon, I look down at the ribbons in my hand. A white and two reds - not bad.

I start to get up because I think the awards are over. I see a volunteer walk over to stand next to the podium with a bunch of medals in her hands. "And now for your All-Around Champions." The announcer says, "In sixth place with a score of 31.50, Marissa Li from Perfect Balance Gymnastics

Academy." I didn't know Marissa did so well. But now that I think back, she didn't fall on anything. She performed all her routines like she always does.

"Way to go, Birthday Girl!" I hear Paige saying as she high fives her. It's her birthday! Maybe I should go to her party and celebrate this awesome day with her. The volunteer directs Marissa to stand on the floor next to the 4th place spot since there is no marker for 6th place. Marissa looks awesome with her bronze medal while 5th through 1st All-Arounders are announced. I wish I could be up there. I guess you have to stay on the stupid beam to get an All-Around medal.

After the All-Around winners jump down, the meet director announces the team scores. We got second place! This *is* out of only three teams, but still, it was our first meet and we got a better team score than someone else.

As soon as awards are over, James comes over to us. "Great day, ladies. I think we got our jitters out and we're going to have a great season. You're free to go home with your parents and I'll see you Monday."

"Okay, thanks, Coach" Trista says, and we all repeat, "Thanks Coach."

Trista turns to me as we walk toward our parents. "That was more fun than I expected it to be!" she exclaims. She is bouncing up and down holding her ribbons. She earned red ribbons for floor and vault and a white one for beam. "How many meets do we have? Like 4? 5? It's not enough. James needs to sign us up for more!" I start laughing; she is such a drama queen, and I love it.

"Oh girls, let's get you on the podium for a picture!" my mom says as she walks up to us. She rounds up the rest of the team. Of course, since it's my mom arranging the picture, she has me stand on the first place spot. She says it's because I'm the shortest, but I'm sure she just wants to see me on the top of the podium. Trista and Alexis climb up next to me and Marissa and Paige are next to them. Pretty soon all of our parents are standing in front of us taking pictures. I feel famous.

Then I hear James laughing, "I think you guys got that shot, let's let another team up there." We jump down and my teammates start heading out with their families.

"See you later today, then?" Trista asks me. When I don't say anything she adds, "Marissa's party?"

"Well, no. I'll see you Monday," I reply.

Trista frowns. "You better tell Marissa."

"Tell me what?" Marissa says, hearing her name. She was standing near-by talking to her mom and sister. Now she is facing us and I can see her beautiful All-Around medal around her neck. I'm happy for Marissa, but I also wish I had a medal around my neck too.

"I can't make your party today," I say quietly.

"Oh, that's too bad," Marissa's mom says, saving me from saying more. "If anything changes you can still stop by, okay?" Marissa's mom says, looking from me to my mom.

"Okay, thanks Kay," my mom answers.

We all start to walk out of the building and I'm glad the awkward moment of telling Marissa I wouldn't be at her party is over. I look down at my ribbons. Today did turn out pretty well and now I get to go to a party.

Chapter 17

Round-off Two Back Handsprings on Floor

After I get home I hang my ribbons on a picture frame, place my blue score card in the top drawer of my dresser, and then I shower. When I get out of the shower I see my mom laid out two outfits on my bed. I get to choose one to wear to

Lily's party. I select a light pink short-sleeve sweater dress with a row of brown hearts along the chest and on the trim at the neck, sleeves, and hem. Perfect for a fall party. Then I pick light pink gymnastics shorts to wear underneath so I can do cartwheels if we get to play outside. I bound down the stairs, grab my brown flats that are by the door, and tell my mom I'm ready for her to do my hair.

"Oh, you look so cute. Good pick on the sweater dress," she compliments. She takes the hair brush I hand her and quickly puts my hair up in a ponytail.

We drive to Lily's party chatting about the meet. "Why did Paige take you away after beam?" she asks.

"James told her to because I was upset."

"Why didn't you come see me if you were upset?"

"James said we shouldn't talk to our parents during a meet," I explain.

"Well, that's silly. I'm your mother. You can talk to me any time you want. I'll talk to James about that before the next meet. You come and see me any time you want, okay?"

"Okay," I say, even though I know I won't do it again. I felt silly after. None of the other girls talked to their moms during the meet. If I'm going to be on a team with older girls, then I better act more grown up.

"Did Paige help you feel better?"

"Yeah, Paige is nice. She helps me, like maybe how a sister would," I say.

"You have a good group of girls on your team," my mom says. We drive in silence for a little while and then my mom says, "Savannah, if you're not having fun at this party, I'll just be shopping down the street. You can call me and I can come get you, okay?"

"Okay, but why wouldn't I have fun?" I ask.

"I hope you do have fun. I'm just saying you can call me."

"Okay," I agree as we pull up to Lily's house.

At Lily's party there are girls everywhere and we are having a great time. We played pin the wand on the fairy, ate cupcakes, opened presents, and now we are outside flying butterfly kites. The grass in her back yard is so fluffy and green and there is so much space. Each of us has a colorful butterfly and we are running back and forth trying to get them to fly.

After a few laps I get tired. My butterfly doesn't want to stay up. I run over and hand my butterfly kite to Lily's mom.

"Mrs. Jones, will you hold this?" I ask, giving her my kite.

"Sure, Savannah, are you done?"

"Yeah, I just want to play on the grass," I explain.

She smiles, "Go for it."

I skip out in the open space and do a round-off back handspring. I love doing gymnastics outside, with the sun and breeze in my face. And tonight is cool, but not cold. *It is perfect*, I think, as I see a few bright yellow leaves flutter around the grass.

"Wow, that was cool," Sarah, Lily's first best friend, says. "Can you do that again?" she asks.

"Sure," I say, and I skip back to the end of the grass to give myself room to do the tumbling pass again. I run and do a round-off back handspring. A few of the other girls notice and come running over.

"Can we see that again? We missed it," says one of the girls that just came over. Lily comes over, since all the girls have stopped playing with their kites and are talking to me.

"I can do it again," I say with a grin. I skip back to the other side of the lawn to do my tumbling pass.

This time I run and do a round-off and two back handsprings. The second back handspring hurts my wrists a little, but it was so fun it was worth it.

The girls are clapping and squealing. "I didn't

know you could do flips like that!" Sarah says.

"They're not flips, they're just back handsprings," Lily corrects. Lily is right so I don't say anything. "Let's see whose kite can go higher."

"But I didn't see her do the flips," another girl says. "Can you do it again?"

I smile and nod. As I am backing up, Lily yells at me, "Why are you ruining my party?"

"I'm just having fun," I defend myself.

"No, you're showing off and now no one wants to fly the pretty butterfly kites. Your butterfly was lame so you decided to ruin it for the rest of us!"

I look at the other girls, waiting for one of them to defend me. But none of them do. Of course they don't, this is Lily. Nobody wants to lose their ranking with her.

"Come on, let's go inside, we can leave the freak to her weird tricks," Lily announces and then she turns and huffs off toward the house. The girls follow her. Megan stands there for a minute watching me. I'm relieved she has decided to stay with me. But then she gives me a sad look, shrugs her shoulders, and turns and follows the group to the house.

Chapter 18

Fish Pose on Beam

I can't believe it. I'm abandoned as a freak for doing gymnastics? For the second time today I feel that stupid lump in my throat as the girls follow Lily inside. I look for Lily's mom, who is nice, to help me. But her mom has gone inside and I'm left all alone. I don't even feel like doing another back handspring, which must mean I feel really bad.

Then I remember my teammates. They would never call me a freak for doing gymnastics on grass on a pretty evening. And they would never call me a show off, because they can do it too.

Now what am I going to do? I'm missing Marissa's party to try to get to know these girls and here I am standing all alone. *What do I do? Go inside and pretend nothing happened and try to be nice to Lily? Or just sit out here until my mom comes to get me? How long is it until this horrible party is over?*

I watch another yellow leaf flutter by and I think about my day. I fell on beam today, but I still got a ribbon on floor and vault. Maybe this problem at the party is like my fall. Maybe I can still go in there and have a good time, like in the meet. I decide that I am going to try again and I begin walking to the house. But I'm dreading getting to the house with each step. *What am I doing? Is this fun? Why is this not fun? If Lily is so cool, why isn't her party fun?* I get to the house and open the door and step inside. I hear girls giggling and my stomach sinks as I understand that this party is fun for everyone except me.

"Hey, freak," Lily says. "You're here just in time to learn you are now tenth. I'm pretty sure party-ruiners should not be fifth." The girls giggle some more. Megan gives me a guilty look, but I know now that she is not going to say anything. I'm not sure what to do. They have made a circle around Lily looking at her new American Girl Doll and I am obviously not invited into that circle. I stare at their backs facing me. My heart feels like it's in my stomach and I can feel my cheeks burning.

I want to disappear.

Then I remember my mom saying I could call her. She can come get me and I can disappear. I wonder if she knew this would happen. How do moms know everything? I decide to go ask Mrs. Jones to call my mom. I happily leave the sight of the closed circle in front of me and wander off to the kitchen where I find Lily's mom cleaning up the cupcake mess we left.

"Mrs. Jones, may I use your phone?" I say, shyly.

"Savannah?" She says with concern, immediately seeing my distress. Which you would think makes me feel better but it makes me even more uncomfortable that I can't hide my feelings.

"What's wrong?" she asks.

Your daughter is a big-fat-meanie-head!

"I just don't feel good. I think I ate too many cupcakes," I say.

"Oh no. Well, of course, you can call your mom," she says, handing me her cell phone.

I dial my mom and she picks up on the first ring. "Deb here," she says.

"Mommy?" I say choking past my famous lump, which grew bigger as soon as I heard my mom's voice.

"Oh honey, what's wrong?"

"I ate too many cupcakes. Can you come get me?"

Chapter 19

Handstand Contest

I decide to wait for my mom outside. I'm sitting in the front yard on a giant rock on the edge of the grass with my knees tucked under my chin and my dress stretched over my legs. When my mom drives up she hops out of the car. "Oh, honey, what happened?"

"I have a tummy ache," I answer, desperately holding on to my pride.

"Okay, let's thank Mrs. Jones and we will be on our way," my mom says. She steps up to the front door and rings the doorbell. I stand behind her and peek around her as Lily's mom answers the door.

"Hi Debbie. Thanks for coming to get her. Sorry I pumped her with too much sugar." She yells over her shoulder, "Lily! Your friend is leaving, get her one of the party favor bags." Lily runs to the door with a basket of clear plastic bags with butterflies on them. They are tied with a pink ribbon and it looks so pretty. I reach out for the bag as Lily smirks at me.

"Sorry you aren't feeling well," she says as sweet as can be and I want to kick her in the shins. I mumble thanks and I see Megan behind her with true concern on her face.

"Bye, Savannah," Megan says. Lily turns and I can see her giving Megan a weird expression. But Megan ignores her and says, "See you Monday."

I nod and turn to my mom's car and walk to

it quickly. I'm so glad to get out of there. It was awful.

My mom gets in the car and says, "You want to tell me what really happened?"

"I have a tummy ache," I insist, mostly because I don't know what else to say.

"Savannah, you have never gotten sick from too much sugar. What happened?" she asks again.

I tell her about how much fun we were having. How we were flying kites on the grass and how all that space just made me want to do gymnastics. And how Lily accused me of showing off and ruining her party. And how now I'm going to be number ten.

"Honey, you shouldn't be ashamed of having fun and doing what you enjoy. And Lily is calling it showing off because she's jealous."

"But I kind of was showing off. I mean, the first one I wasn't, but then the girls asked to see more and I was showing off for them."

"Savannah, it's okay to show your friends what you can do. If Lily was good at drawing, would you look at her drawings?" she asks.

"Yeah," I answer in a pouty voice.

"Would it mean she was showing off or just sharing her drawing with you?"

"Just sharing, I guess."

"Well, you were just sharing what you like to do with your friends. And by the way, Lily should not be ranking her friends like that."

"I know," I say, and I really do know, but I'm not sure how to change it. I look down at my hands and notice the party favor bag in my lap. I untie the pink ribbon and look inside. I see flavored lip balm, gum, candy, colorful plastic bracelets, beaded bracelets, and some plastic rings. I start giggling. Just like Trista said, *you might get some cool bracelets or something out of it in the goodie bag.* Trista can make me laugh even when we're not together. Then all of a sudden I'm ashamed I chose Lily's party over Marissa's party. Marissa has been nice to me the whole time I have known her. She has never ranked me or made me feel bad. And I went to a mean girl's party just to be liked at school. What a mess.

"Mom, is it too late to go to Marissa's house? Do you think my team will still be there?"

My mom looks up at me through the rear view mirror of the car. "It might not be, let me call Kay," she says, pulling over. My mom dials Kay's number and they have a quick conversation. I can tell I'm going to get to go to Marissa's party by the time they hang up.

When I arrive at Marissa's house it's almost dark, but the girls are out front having a handstand contest on the grass. I bound out of the car and run over to them. Trista sees me first. "You came!" she says, as she runs to me and gives me a hug.

"Happy Birthday, Marissa, sorry I didn't get here sooner," I apologize.

"Thanks! You're just in time for one last handstand contest before it gets too dark."

"But really quick," I say, "before handstands.

I brought you guys something." I open up the butterfly goodie bag and dig in it for the bracelets.

The girls are standing around me in a circle. I give them each a bracelet.

"So you did get some cool swag," Trista comments, slipping the blue bracelet on her wrist. "Was it worth it?" she asks.

"Not really, but at least we got cool bracelets out of it," I say with a grin. Trista laughs, knowing I got this from her.

"Okay guys, we're almost out of light," Paige says, putting on the yellow bracelet.

"Okay," I say, backing up and kicking off my shoes to get ready for a handstand. We spread out in a line so we don't hit each other if we fall.

Marissa says, "Hands up! Stands up!" We all kick up to a handstand. Alexis and I fall right away and start giggling. Alexis stands up and starts tickling Trista's feet.

"Hey, what are you doing?" Trista laughs as she falls.

"Just helping the birthday girl win," Alexis explains. Then she skips over to Paige and starts in on her until she falls.

"Hey!" Paige complains, "You made me fall!"

"No, I didn't," Alexis denies, "If you were concentrating, it wouldn't have mattered. Hey, birthday girl, you won!" she yells over to Marissa.

"I heard all of that," Marissa says, coming down out of her handstand. "I never win," she grins, "you must have had something to do with it, Lex."

We all start laughing, "Happy Birthday, you won," Alexis insists.

I love these girls. There is nothing better than gym friends.

Up Next?
Paige's Story
Book 3 in the Perfect Balance Gymnastics Series

Dance is the Secret Event

Chapter 1

"You have a new dance coach today,"
James tells us. I'm stretching on the floor with my
Level 3 teammates. We are listening to our coach,
James, explain what we are going to be working
on today.

"Why do we even need dance?" Trista asks.

"Because dance can be the difference

between polished versus sloppy gymnastics. The difference between winning and losing," he says.

If James says dance is how you win, then I'm going pay attention in dance class. I want to place in the All-Around at our State Meet. I really think I can do it. I placed in the All-Around at the last three meets of the season.

"Today you are going to start with the dance rotation, so go get your tights on and head upstairs," he orders.

We get up out of our splits and go into the lobby where our bags are in the cubbies along the wall. I get to my cubby first and pull out my gym bag. I rummage through and find my tights and ballet slippers. I sit down to put on my tights over my leotard as I listen to my teammates talk.

"Do you have the wolf Beanie Boo?" Alexis asks Marissa.

"I have one that's a Huskie, not a wolf. His name is Slush, is that the one you're thinking of?" Marissa asks.

"I think so, gray and white, Drew has it. It's so cute, that's my favorite one," Alexis says.

"Is there a bunny Beanie Boo?" Savannah asks.

Since I could care less about Beanie Boos I don't join the conversation. I stand up and finish pulling on my tights. Then I go to the stairs and up to the dance area. As much as I love my teammates, sometimes their chatter seems childish to me. After all, I'm two years older than most of them.

I walk into the dance studio and look at my reflection in the floor to ceiling dance room mirrors. I don't really look like a gymnast because I have on pink tights and black ballet slippers. But I don't look like a dancer either because my tights are pulled over my leotard. We do this so we can get back to our gymnastics workout faster after the dance rotation.

I walk to the middle of the room, there are mirrors and ballet barres on three walls and a window to the training area on the far left wall.

What would it be like to be a real dancer? I wonder as a pull my hair up from a pony tail into a tucked under half pony tail. This makes my crazy hair look like it's in a bun. I have bright red hair with tiny curls that spring up everywhere. No amount of gel, spray, frizz ease, or cream will put my curls down.

I can hear my teammates running up the stairs like a herd of elephants. For a bunch of petite little third graders, they sure do make a lot of noise.

"Does Megan only ignore you at school?" I hear Trista ask Savannah as they stubble through the doorway.

"Yes, but I know she doesn't like to," Savannah answers.

"Oh, hey Paige, you got up here fast," Trista says. Not really, they were just slow getting on their tights because they were busy talking.

I shrug in response as they start doing gymnastics poses in front of the mirrors.

Alexis runs over to the viewing window on the left wall, "Look at the boys' team tumble, they're so sloppy," she says. This makes all the girls run over and look out the window.

"Hello girls," we hear. We all turn to see our new ballet teacher. She is the tallest thinnest woman I have ever seen. She is wearing pink tights with a black leotard over them. Around her waist is a black transparent knee length flowing skirt. She makes our tights over our leotards look kind of lame. Her hair is in a perfect dark blond bun and she has so much grace just walking over to the front of the room.

"I am your new Madame." *Our what?* James said we had a new dance teacher, but I assumed she would be a coach. This lady is not a gymnastics coach. Most gymnastics coaches used to be gymnasts. They are usually short and muscly, not tall and willowy. "I am from the Salt Lake City Ballet Company and I will be teaching you traditional ballet." *Isn't that what we have been doing?*

"Kathryn hired me to prepare you for the State Meet you have coming up," she continues. "Why don't you each take your place at the barre and we will begin with tendus."

My team is standing stunned by the window. Her announcement to begin brakes the trance and the girls start being their lively selves again.

Trista cartwheels over to the other side of the room while Savannah skips next to her. Marissa runs over to the barre at the back of the room, and Alexis sashays over to Marissa's barre. I look around and the only barre left is the one by the window, so I walk over to it and stand next to the barre by myself.

About the Author

Melisa Torres grew up in San Jose, California. She trained at Almaden Valley Gymnastics Club where she competed in USA Gymnastics' Junior Olympic program for ten years. Melisa then went to compete for Utah State University where she was a two-time Academic All-American and team captain.

Melisa currently lives in Utah and is a single mother to two active boys. Their favorite things to do together are skiing, swimming, going to the library, and dancing in the kitchen.

Read all the books in the Perfect Balance Gymnastics Series!

PERFECT BALANCE GYMNASTICS SERIES
Grace and Confidence for Life!

MELISATORRES.COM
*For unique gymnastics gifts,
book signing dates, and to apply for our
Reader of the Month Program.*

FACEBOOK.COM/PBGSERIES
*For articles about gymnastics and
updates on new releases.*

@PERFECTBALANCEGYMBOOKS
*Following gymnasts and young writers to
give encouragement and inspiration*

Made in the USA
Middletown, DE
05 February 2021